Santa Clauses

Short Poems from the North Pole

by **Bob Raczka**

illustrated by
Chuck Groenink

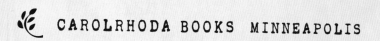
CAROLRHODA BOOKS MINNEAPOLIS

To every child who finds it hard to
sleep on Christmas Eve
—B.R.

In memory of Aunt Mia, who taught me
what Christmas is all about
—C.G.

Text copyright © 2014 by Bob Raczka
Illustrations copyright © 2014 by Chuck Groenink

Carolrhoda Books
A division of Lerner Publishing Group, Inc.
241 First Avenue North
Minneapolis, MN 55401 USA

For reading levels and more information, look up this title at
www.lernerbooks.com.

Library of Congress Cataloging-in-Publication Data

Raczka, Bob.
   (Poems. Selections)
   Santa clauses: Short poems from the North Pole / By Bob Raczka ; Illustrated by Chuck
Groenink.
      pages   cm
   ISBN 978-1-4677-1805-9 (lib. bdg. : alk. paper)
   ISBN 978-1-4677-4621-2 (eBook)
   I. Groenink, Chuck, ill. II. Title.
PS3618.A346S26 2014
811'.6—dc23

2013030819

Manufactured in the United States of America
1 - DP - 7/15/14

Santa is a man of many talents. He's a toymaker, a reindeer trainer, a sleigh pilot, and a world traveler. But did you know he is also a poet?

Years ago, Mrs. Claus gave him a book of haiku, a Japanese form of poetry. Each haiku is just three lines long, with five syllables in the first line, seven in the second, and five in the third. Santa loved these poems. He was even inspired to write his own.

Now you can peek at Santa's haiku, one for each day from December 1 to December 25, and catch a glimpse of life at the North Pole. Hear the snow crunch. Smell the gingerbread. And see a side of Santa you've never seen before.

December 1st
Wishes blowing in
from my overfilled mailbox—
December's first storm.

December 2nd
A snow hare admires
my cute little snow elf, his
nose especially.

December 3rd
Mrs. Claus making
an angel, becoming a
little girl again.

December 4th
Sprinkling sand on my
snow-covered steps, thinking of
nutmeg on eggnog.

December 5th
I untie knots in
strings of lights while Mrs. Claus
ties bows on presents.

December 6th
Replacing bad bulbs
with good ones, moving naughty
names to the nice list.

December 7th
Navigating by
the stars, Comet and I drag
this year's tree homeward.

December 8th
Just after moonrise
I meet my tall, skinny twin—
"Good evening, shadow."

December 9th
Elves pounding, sawing
and sanding, a holiday
concert performance.

December 10th
The north wind and I
whistling to "Let It Snow!"
on the radio.

December 11th
Kisses from Mrs.
Claus under the mistletoe
tickle like snowflakes.

December 12th
Stringing popcorn to hang on the tree, one for the string and two for me.

December 13th
Mother Nature trims
her trees with icicles, snow,
pinecones, and moonlight.

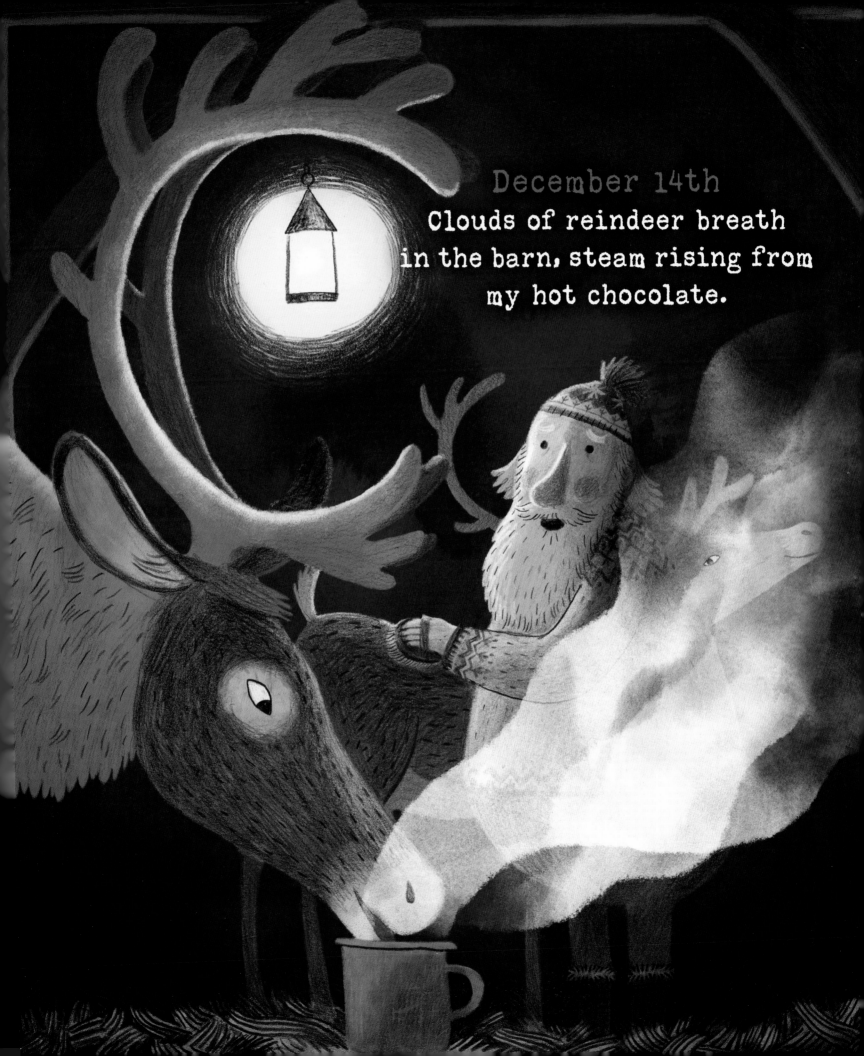

December 14th
Clouds of reindeer breath
in the barn, steam rising from
my hot chocolate.

December 15th
One hundred strings of
outdoor lights can't compete with
tonight's aurora.

December 16th

Dripping snow freezes
into icicles; cookies
bake in the oven.

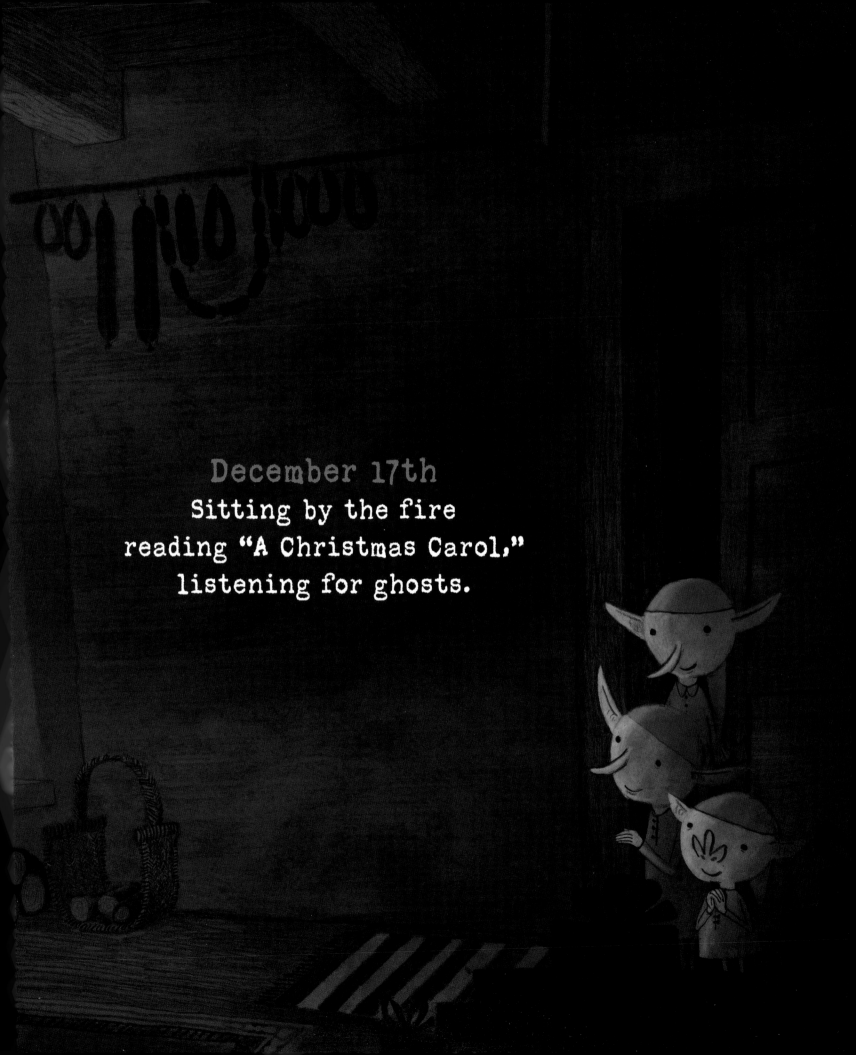

December 17th
Sitting by the fire
reading "A Christmas Carol,"
listening for ghosts.

December 18th
Mrs. Claus and I
wrapped neatly in our bed quilts—
matching packages.

December 19th
Fat white fox at the
salt lick, while I lick the stripes
off my candy cane.

December 20th
Workshop storm warning
in effect, heavy sawdust
accumulation.

December 21st
Silent night, except
for the distant carolers
howling at the moon.

December 22nd
Reading the reindeer's
favorite bedtime story,
my cold nose glows red.

December 24th

Which is packed tighter, the sack full of toys or the red suit full of me?

December 25th
From my flying sleigh,
I look down on fields and towns—
a toy train layout.